Nick Butterworth

A Flying Visit

HarperCollins *Children's Books*

For Ben…This book
was made for you with

LˇVOˇ

Dad

First published in hardback in Great Britain by HarperCollins *Children's Books* in 2021

HarperCollins *Children's Books* is a division of HarperCollins*Publishers* Ltd
1 London Bridge Street, London SE1 9GF

www.harpercollins.co.uk

HarperCollins*Publishers*
1st Floor, Watermarque Building, Ringsend Road, Dublin 4, Ireland

1 3 5 7 9 10 8 6 4 2

Text and illustrations copyright © Nick Butterworth 2021

ISBN: 978-0-00-845562-0

Printed in China

On a fine autumn day, Percy the park keeper might catch a glimpse of his friend, the hedgehog, nestled comfortably among the mossy roots of his favourite tree.

He seems to be dreaming, though his eyes are open. Percy will smile and tiptoe past. Only someone who doesn't know the hedgehog would disturb him here…

The hedgehog lay on his back beneath a giant conker tree that stood where Percy's park met the world beyond.

He gazed up through the tree's bare branches to the birds circling high in the autumn sky.

"Oh, to be able to fly." He sighed. "Wouldn't that be wonderful!" His eyes began to close, but his daydream was interrupted by a voice.

"No…no…no…no…no…" then, THUMP!

The tree shook and conkers thudded to the ground all around the hedgehog. He quickly rolled himself into a ball and didn't dare peep through his fingers, until the voice came again…

"Hello."

Hanging upside down in front of the hedgehog was a strange bird. It was tangled up in what looked like a washing line and was going up and down like a yo-yo.

"I'm Carla. Nice coat you've got."

"Er…thank you. Glad you like it. I'm a hedgehog. It looks like you've got yourself into a spot of bother."

"A bit," said the bird, still going up and down. "Any chance you could…help?"

"I'll try," said the hedgehog, "but I think I should tell Percy. He'll know what—"

"No, no, please, Hedgehog! Don't tell!"

"Oh, but," the hedgehog began, "Percy is—"

"No, no, no!" Carla pleaded.

"Oh dear. Please, please don't be upset," said the hedgehog. "I will help you. What do you need? Are you hungry?"

"Mmmm, yes. A bit peckish – ha ha!"

The hedgehog thought for a moment. "How about a sandwich?"

"Oooooh yes, A nice, tasty sandwich. Very good," said Carla.

"OK," said the hedgehog, "wait there."

Carla had stopped bouncing up and down and was now slowly turning from left to right and back again.

"Right," she said as the hedgehog scampered off. "I'll wait here."

"Where am I going to get a sandwich?" said the hedgehog to himself. "Percy's the only one who makes sandwiches, but I can't tell him about C— Owwwwwww!"

The hedgehog caught his foot in some brambles,
tripped and found himself spinning through the air…

Percy had been working nearby and had stopped for lunch. He wasn't expecting the hedgehog to drop in – especially on top of his last sandwich.

"Hello!" said Percy. "Where did you spring from?"

The hedgehog's spines were stuck in the sandwich. He struggled to get up.

"Hold on," Percy chuckled. "I'll help you. I'll just get my gardening gloves, if you don't mind."

Percy disappeared, but the hedgehog continued to struggle. With a great effort, he managed to roll off Percy's lunch table, on to his feet and away.

Carla was glad to see the hedgehog again and even more pleased to see the sandwich.

"Oh – that's good! Very clever. That coat comes in handy, hey?"

"Er, yes." The hedgehog paused. "Do you think you could eat the sandwich where it is?"

"Of course!" said Carla.

The hedgehog turned his back, and Carla quickly polished off every crumb.

"My! You were hungry!" said the hedgehog.

"Oh yes," said Carla. "Always hungry. That's how I ended up here."

"What happened?" the hedgehog asked.

"This morning, I spied breakfast. Near some washing.
I swooped, but the washing went flappy-flap.
Missed breakfast.
Hit the post."

"And that's how you got tangled up in the washing line?"

"That's right. I'm strong. I got away, but the washing wanted to come too. Then…" Carla paused. "I got lost."

"I thought birds never get lost," said the hedgehog.

"That's right. They don't. But still…I did. Must be the bump. On my head."

"Oh dear! You're hurt!" said the hedgehog. "Is it painful?"

"A bit. Yes."

"I'll get a plaster from Percy!" said the hedgehog.

"Oh no! Don't tell. No…no…no…!"

But the hedgehog had already set off.

When Percy returned with his gardening gloves, the hedgehog had vanished. Instead, he found the fox and the badger.

"Hello, you two," he said. "You haven't seen the hedgehog and…a sandwich, have you?"

"The hedgehog?" said the badger.

"A sandwich?" said the fox.

"Yes," Percy answered.

"No," the fox and badger said together.

"Pity. They were both here and now they're both not here."

"Was there only one sandwich?" the fox asked.

"Yes," said Percy. "And only one hedgehog."

"We'll keep an eye out for them," said the badger.

"Please be in," the hedgehog panted as he ran up the steps to Percy's hut.

But Percy wasn't in, because he was out, looking for the hedgehog.

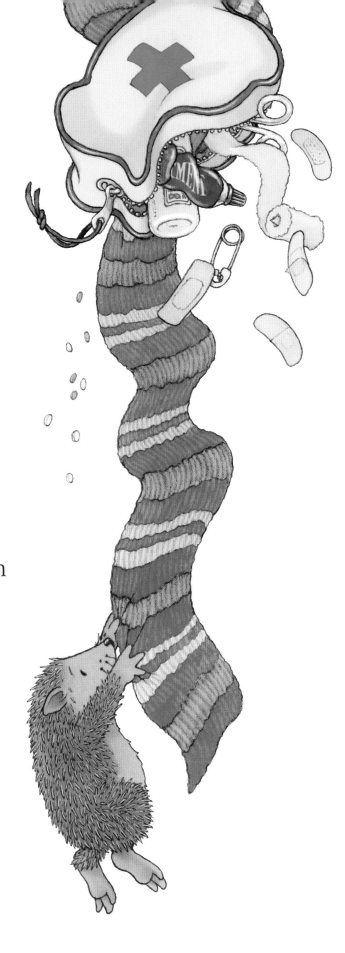

"Oh dear. I wonder where Percy keeps plasters. I think he has a special bag. Ah! There it is!"

Percy's first-aid bag was sitting on top of his scarf, which was hanging over the edge of his table. It was too high to reach.

"I wonder if I…" He gave a tug.

The scarf and the bag slipped from the table, and as they hit the floor everything in the bag spilled out in front of him.

The hedgehog chose three plasters and away he went.

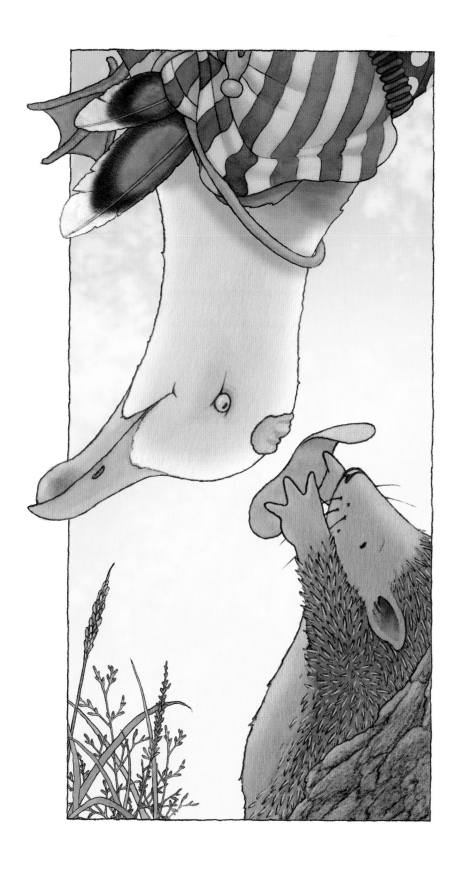

The hedgehog found Carla where he had left her.

"Good, you're still here," he said.

"Oh yes. Still here."

As carefully as he could, the hedgehog put three plasters on Carla's head.

"How does that feel? Better?"

"Er…mmm. A bit better."

"Can I help?" a kind voice asked.

The hedgehog jumped and Carla looked worried.

"Who is this?" she whispered.

The hedgehog beamed. "This is Percy!"

"Is Percy OK?" Carla asked.

"Yes," said the hedgehog. "Percy is OK."

Carefully, Percy untangled Carla from the washing line and looked at the bump on her head.

"It's lovely to meet you, er…?"

"I'm Carla. Lucky I landed here. Lucky I met Hedgehog. He gave me a nice, tasty sandwich."

"Ah, did he?" Percy smiled. "Well, let's see what else we can do to get you back on your feet."

"Oh yes," said Carla. "See, I've got to get going. You know. Must fly."

The hedgehog sighed. "Oh, I wish I could fly, like you."

"Like me," Carla laughed. "But not fly into things, hey?"

"We could fly together," said the hedgehog.

"Wouldn't that be something!" said Carla.

"Go whenever you want," said Percy. "But it might be good to get your strength back first."

"I'm strong," said Carla. "Still, maybe I could stay. Just till tomorrow."

It was three days later, early in the morning, when Percy and a group of old friends, and one new friend, gathered by the conker tree.

"Are you quite sure about this, Carla?" Percy asked.

"Oh yes," said Carla. "I'm sure."

Percy turned to the hedgehog. "And you're sure too?"

"Oh yes, yes!" the hedgehog squealed.

"All right," said Percy. "Let's go!"

Carla spread out her great wings, and with three beats she was in the air. And with three beats more...

So was the hedgehog!

As they rose together, higher and higher, the sky grew bigger and the world below seemed suddenly small.

"How do you like flying?" asked Carla.

"It's…it's…WONDERFUL!" the hedgehog gasped. "I can see the whole park! There's Percy's hut. And look! There they all are. They're so tiny. Hello! Hello! I'm flying! I'M A BIRD!"

"Heh, heh! You are one brave hedgehog," Carla laughed as she swooped and dived.

At last, Carla slowed to
hover in the breeze.
"Ready now?" she asked.
The hedgehog breathed in
and took hold of two strings.
"Ready!" he said, and pulled
hard on the strings…

At once, the scarf that had been the hedgehog's seat flapped wildly in the wind and the rushing air streamed past his ears and whiskers. Then, everything changed…

The scarf opened into a parachute! The wind stopped and the hedgehog began to float gently down,

down,

down…

"See you another day!" he called to Carla.

"Yes!" she called back. "I'll see you soon!"

The hedgehog watched his new friend grow smaller and smaller until she disappeared into the enormous sky.

Percy reached out and one very happy hedgehog sailed safely into his hands.

"What an adventure you've had," he chuckled. "And all before breakfast! You must be hungry. What would you like to eat?"

The hedgehog smiled. "Do you know what I'd really like…?"

And together everyone said,

"A NICE, TASTY SANDWICH!"